THE PHANTOM MAGICIAN AND THE TIGER PALACE

VIVEK CHOWTHRI

Inkfeathers Publishing

www.inkfeathers.com

The Phantom Magician and the Tiger Palace
by Vivek Chowthri
Print Edition

First Published in India in 2021
Inkfeathers Publishing
New Delhi 110095

ISBN 978-93-90882-02-1

www.inkfeathers.com

Dedicated to

My Parents, My Wife, My Siblings,

My Relatives, My Friends and

My Newborn Prince

Sai Sarvesh

CONTENTS

PREFACE

First and foremost, I want to thank each and everyone who cared to read my book for spending their fruitful time. And spoiler alert: this preface is going to be slightly long as I don't know whether I would write another book, so I will try to mention as many things as possible. Hence, if you skip the preface and get straight to the story, I understand and respect that.

I, E. Vivek Chowthri, am an Engineer by degree. Now, I understand the question that may arise in your mind, 'Why do Engineers always do something not related to Engineering?' I can't give you a straight-forward answer to that question, but the answer that pops in my mind is that it is because a majority of those who pursue Engineering don't want to pursue it in the first place. They dream of something else, yet get locked up in Engineering.

In my case, I wanted to be an Animator but somehow got mixed up in Aeronautical Engineering. The moment anyone would hear I got a seat in Aeronautical Engineering; they would always say that I would travel to foreign countries and do all kinds of somersaults in jets like a pilot would do. But in reality, Aeronautical Engineering is very different from Pilot Training. People never understand that.

To achieve a career in Aeronautical, according to me, the

following things were required: time, money, and mainly; unbiased, non-deviated dedication. When I analysed my schedule, it was well and good until my Father passed away. It got worse when I got married. Money was always partly a problem for me. Again, I stress, *partly*. As I grew up, my needs and expectations surpassed my age and demanded more money. At one point, I was given a common answer that if I want something, I must get it with my own hard-earned money. When I started to earn, the ratio of my expenses exceeded my salary like the Tamil song, *"Varavu Etanna, Selavu Pathanna..."*

So, I had to sacrifice the main thing for which I had started to work to maintain my basic medical, vehicle, fuel, grocery, and many other expenses. Next, as you may understand, I never had unbiased dedication. No matter what or how hard I tried, my mind always got deviated to the Animation and Movie Industry. But I also want to mention that I had scored approximately 86% in my first year of Engineering. I didn't study for myself, but I studied hard for the fees paid by my parents. The main reason I got deviated more was due to the lack of encouragement and support when I fell. All my friends and staff would support me in every step of mine, yet, if the right kind of support is not received from the right people at the right time, you would end up as a half-baked failure.

Here, half-baked indicates both success and failure in equal measures. But according to the society we live in, even the second place is considered a failure. So, I asked NEXT just like *Veerabagu* in the Tamil Movie *Giri,* but I got the same reply which Arjun would say in the movie from my mind.

One day, my friend, *Mr. Sampath* told me that no matter how hard we cry, curse, blame or do anything in protest to a problem, only we have to face it and overcome it. So stop protesting and start solving. Those words somehow had a slow-poison effect on me.

By the time I had completed the degree I had already missed my train, in my case, flight. Then, I joined Animation as a side course. Then, I decided to enter the Filmmaking Industry. Now, I am still trying. After my father passed away, I started a CAD and Animation Training Institute named *Evolve Creative Academy* in August 2016 with a minimum budget I could attain at that time.

This book was started as a practice session for both story writing in Movie Industry and Journal Publishing in Aeronautical Engineering on the suggestion of my friend, *Mrs. S. Vaisali*. I started this book two years back in late December 2018. I would regularly complete a chapter and send it to her. Slowly, I started sending it to many people and they sent it to their friends and colleagues. But in the next few months, people stopped asking me for story updates, my writing got slowed. When I got married in June 2019, my priorities completely got changed and I never opened the story.

In the meantime, my brother from other parents and to be guru, *Mr. Athiyan Athirai* started to shoot his Tamil film, *Irandam Ulaga Porin Kadaisi Gundu*. So, I went to the shooting during the schedule near my hometown. I visited the spot regularly and used to watch and learn how film making is done. When the shooting was over, I took up a job as a Supervising Engineer in a company called *Southern Tech Equipments*.

In my whole life, very few people have understood me for who I am; one among the few was my boss, *Mr. Hem Kumar*. He gave me full freedom and encouraged me to do everything I wished for, as long as I didn't deviate and delay his work and that of the company.

Now let's catch up with those who have skipped the preface. Hope you enjoy the story! Awaiting your response!

1

THE JOURNEY BEGINS

The pleasant morning woke up the town of Amirthaveli. It was 7:00 a.m. when the doorbell rang. Shenba Nagulan went for the door in his nightclothes. A strange man was standing there, looking dull and tired. "Does 'The Phantom Magician' live here?" he asked Shenba as soon as he opened the door. That name was given by the locals to Shenba for his paranormal mystery-solving abilities. "That would be me, come inside." Shenba said, inviting the man inside.

Shenba fumbled around in a haste to clear the room and made space for the stranger to sit. "So, what brings you here?" he asked, while serving a cup of tea. Out of the corner of his eye, he noticed that the stranger's hands were twitching and covered in bruises. "I am from a village called Parangikadu," he said, handing a letter to Shenba. It was from his friend Tharanga Rajan. The letter read:

Dear Shenba,

How are you? It was hard to reach you through any other means since you don't carry a mobile phone. I'm in trouble. To be precise, my whole village is in trouble. There have been certain incidents in my village. People are going missing every week, especially children. My people are afraid and believe it might be something extremely ghastly. Most of them are scared about their own and their children's lives, and now the village is almost deserted. If this continues, all of us would have to vacate or we would go missing like the others. Please come as soon as possible. We really need your help.

Your Friend,
Tharanga Rajan
30.11.2018

"What's your name?" Shenba asked, looking up from the letter. "I am Mannaiyan, a farmer." he said. When asked about the village's condition, he broke down. Shenba consoled him till he finished drinking tea. Getting up from his chair, Mannaiyan bid adieu despite Shenba's insistence over him staying. After Mannaiyan was gone, Shenba came to the big verandah outside. From the verandah, one could see all of Amirthaveli.

He was a comic geek and avidly read paranormal stories. It was this fascination which had made him take inspiration for his work from pieces like "Doctor Strange" and "Constantine." He lost track of time watching the beauty of Amirthaveli while thinking of Rajan's letter. It was only when the clock struck at noon that he realized that he'd forgotten to take his bath and breakfast that morning. Quickly freshening up, he went to a hotel for lunch.

Afterwards, when the sun was slightly down, he went to the library. He gathered as much information about the village. He also got some books on ghosts, spirits, and souls. To his surprise, there were no newspaper articles regarding these missing people.

Baffled, he left the library and checked the bus timing for the village. The last bus would depart from Amirthaveli at 8:00 p.m.

He went home and started packing things for his journey. After dinner, he went to the bus stop, only to find that the bus's engine was damaged, which made the authorities cancel the last schedule. Taking a seat, Shenba sat and thought of whether to return home or look for an alternate mode of transport.

Just then, a fellow passenger asked him his destination and offered him a ride to a nearer place from where he could travel by foot. Shenba accepted the offer and boarded the old car. The passenger introduced himself as Chandrakumar. He came from a village called Puliyanur, which was separated from two mountains and a forest from Parangikadu. He was well-educated and in his mid-30's. He worked as a Manager in Amirthaveli.

Chandrakumar explained the reason for the names of both the villages. As Parangikadu was at the bottom of the mountain near the forest, it was named as such "Parangi—rock or mountain; Kadu—forest". Puliyanur was named after its reputation for frequent sightings of tigers. Local folklore even had songs about "Half tiger, Half human" people and their palace which lay somewhere in the forest in between the mountains. That woke a sense of curiosity in Shenba.

Chandrakumar asked Shenba to stay in his village till morning, as it was not safe to travel to Parangikadu through the forest at night, which was the only route to the village. After some serious thought, Shenba agreed to spend the night in Puliyanur.

At half-past eleven, the car took a turn on a small road off the highway. The road had not been maintained, so they had to drive slowly. The road being narrow, the bushes on the side of the road started to hit up against the windows of the car. A thorn bush caused a slight tear in Shenba's left-hand shirt sleeve. The ride turned bumpy due to the horrifying potholes, which made Shenba hit his head against the car roof several times.

Chandrakumar laughed at Shenba's misery. Shenba wondered how people could drive on this road. At around midnight, the car crossed a mountain which Chandrakumar had earlier mentioned to Shenba. Shenba realized that Chandrakumar wasn't lying about the density of the forest.

Trees and bushes covered the forest in a way that even sunlight and moonlight couldn't shine through some areas of the forest. They had crossed the mountain about a mile when Shenba saw a board reading "Puliyanur Welcomes You."

A few feet away from the board stood a statue of 'Aiyanaar—God of Protection'. The car moved towards the village. There was dead silence. The sounds of insects and cattle could be heard amidst the car sound. A few passers-by sleeping outside their houses slightly opened their eyes to acknowledge their arrival.

They finally stopped outside a big house surrounded by fields. A small light bulb flashed on the top of the front door. An old lady in her late sixties opened the door and invited Chandrakumar. Another lady in her late thirties peeked through the door.

Chandrakumar introduced Shenba to his mother and wife. His mother asked them to sleep and talk later in the morning. She showed Shenba to a small room with a bed at one end of the house. There was a single window opposite the door and some old trunk boxes on the floor.

There was a photo of a youngster in the room. He appeared to be in his early twenties. There were some clothes on the shelf, probably belonging to the fellow in the photograph. Chandrakumar's wife brought a water bottle and a glass for Shenba. After she went, Shenba looked at the watch. It was almost 1:00 a.m. Lying in bed, he pondered over the day's events, and finally giving in to his exhaustion, drifted off into a deep sleep.

2

MISSING BROTHER

In the morning, at 6.00 AM, the sounds of goats bleating, cows mooing and cocks crowing made Shenba wake up from his sleep. This was a very new experience to him, as he was used to the usual din of a busy town. He got up and was making his bed when he heard a knock on the door. When he opened it, a lady, probably a housemaid, was standing there with a cup of coffee.

She seemed to be in her late 40's. She said, "Ayya is waiting for you in the *muttram* (Open space before the house)". Shenba nodded and took the coffee from her hands. He noticed the same kind of bruises on her hands as on Mannaiyan's hands. He drank the coffee and went to the *muttram*. There, Chandrakumar was feeding the animals while ordering the servants to do other chores.

When he saw Shenba, he wished him and asked him to grab a chair and sit. After washing his hands, Chandrakumar sat near Shenba. He told him that the bus would be crossing their village to Parangikadu at 8.30 AM. He ordered the maid for a coffee as well.

Only then Shenba remembered that Chandrakumar never asked anything about his purpose of the visit. He became a bit suspicious and wary. 'What kind of man invites a stranger to stay in his place without asking any details about the stranger?' he thought to himself.

Chandrakumar noticed a change in his demeanour and enquired, "Is something wrong?" Shenba hesitantly told him about his suspicion. Chandrakumar laughed and asked Shenba to tell his purpose first before giving away any sort of explanation. The maid entered the room, a coffee cup in her hands. When Shenba disclosed his intention to solve the mystery of the missing people, the maid dropped the cup in shock and started crying, her body trembling in shock and fainted on the spot.

Shenba immediately got up and tried to offer help, but Chandrakumar asked the other servants to tend to the maid. "Please don't worry. Take your seat. I'll tell you about myself." he said. He started introducing his family. The old woman, who appeared to be in her 60's, was his mother. Her name was Periyachi.

Gunalini, a woman in her 30's, was his wife. They had a daughter, Gunachandra, named after both of their first names. She was three years old. Chandrakumar had a brother named Indrakumar, who was pursuing his degree in the city. His father had passed away a few years ago due to illness.

After his father's demise, he discontinued his studies and came back to the village to take care of the family business and chores because of Chandrakumar's job in Amirthaveli. Though the elder brother insisted Indrakumar on continuing his studies, he came back anyways. Their family business was to supply vegetables from their farm to the nearby villages, especially Parangikadu.

They had a tractor which helped Indrakumar in supplying the goods. While going via bus or any other vehicle, the route to Parangikadu was around the mountains which was around 6 to 8 miles long. Whereas while walking, the easy path was through the forest in the mountains, which was just 3 miles.

But this path was dangerous when traveling alone, as there were tigers and other vicious animals in the forest. Safe travel could only be ensured if there were 3 or more travellers. A few months ago, Indrakumar went to supply vegetables to Parangikadu and never returned. It was on the day of their daughter's third birthday. He was really close to her. He went in their tractor but returned through the forest alone since the tractor broke down in Parangikadu.

This was the main reason why Chandrakumar helped Shenba in the first place. As Chandrakumar was explaining, Shenba got even more questions popping in his mind.

Why did Chandrakumar offer me a ride? Why did the maid faint? Why did Indrakumar return through the forest even when he was well aware of the situation? Was he dead? Or did he just go missing? Was there any link of this incident to the Parangikadu missing cases? Did they even contact the local authorities?

Without minding a thoughtful Shenba, Chandrakumar continued his explanation. The maid, Parvatham, was from Parangikadu. There had been some strange things that started to happen there. The people of the village either went mad or went missing. The maid was one among the people who went mad.

The bruise marks in her hands were due to tying her up in special chains that were purified with the holy water of the gods. Suddenly, Shenba deduced that Mannaiyan was also one of the victims who went mad. That mess in the village made outsiders afraid about entering Parangikadu. That effect was intense in

Puliyanur because as soon as the trouble started in Parangikadu, the sightings of tigers in Puliyanur began to reduce at some point to completely none.

The reason why Indrakumar was still delivering the supplies was due to the requisition from his friend over that village, Tharanga Rajan. Shenba was dumbstruck on hearing that, as Rajan was the person who asked him to come over there. Shenba asked whether they had filed any complaints with the police. Chandrakumar nodded positively.

The police had closed the case as they had found some torn clothes with some blood on them inside the forest. It was a piece of cloth that Indrakumar was wearing on the day he went missing. The police said he must have gotten killed by the tigers and the case was closed as 'presumed dead'.

In Parangikadu missing cases, no complaints had been filed as people were afraid that something might happen to them if they had filed any complaint. The police were not ready to file the complaint from anyone other than the Parangikadu people.

When enquired, they acted normal as if nothing had happened there. That was the reason for Parvatham fainting. When she woke up, she pleaded with Shenba not to pursue the case as she did not want to meddle with any kind of superior things. Gunalini consoled her. Shenba asked Chandrakumar about the news reporters, and a moment of silence ensued.

Chandrakumar and Shenba went to the backside of the house. There was a small house with closed windows. The door was locked. A servant gave Chandrakumar a set of keys. Chandrakumar proceeded to unlock the door.

When Shenba looked inside, he saw an average heighted man with a piece of charcoal in his hands. The walls of the room were full of scribbles. The scribbles were mostly in the shape of a tiger face or something related to tigers.

Shenba looked at Chandrakumar. Chandrakumar told him that he was the reporter who came to investigate the missing persons. Within a few days in Parangikadu, he went mad and started to blabber incessantly.

The only difference from other people who had gone mad was that he did not expose any kind of rude behaviour. Other people started attacking normal people which was the reason they were tied up. But that guy never attacked anybody, instead started saying something about some strange palace in the forest.

As there were no proofs available for any kind of palace in the forest, Shenba examined the room for any kind of evidence that might help him for his investigation.

The reporter started screaming, “TIGER PEOPLE”. Shenba went near the reporter, as he was shouting that they were coming back to reclaim their homep(a)lace. Shenba looked into the reporter’s eyes, they were dilated bloodshot.

Shenba looked around where he found a piece of paper.

He asked the reporter to draw what he saw. He drew something and again went to the walls for drawing more tiger heads. Shenba and Chandrakumar saw the paper, nothing was clear.

But Chandrakumar pointed to an oval shape that was similar to a lake inside the forest. “SO THAT’S IT!” Shenba shouted. That drawing was a map of the forest. To be precise, it was a mere depiction similar to a map. Shenba collected all the papers in the room. He also found a Tiger headed pendant. He enquired Chandrakumar about the pendant.

But he didn’t have any kind of knowledge about that pendant. Shenba went to the reporter and mildly asked him about the pendant. He pointed next to the lake on the paper before again scribbling on the walls. Shenba and Chandrakumar left the house. Shenba was pondering throughout the events that had happened.

Chandrakumar asked whether Shenba had found anything. Shenba didn't reply. When they reached the front of the house, Periyachi asked them both to come over for breakfast within 15 minutes. Shenba went in for a bath and packed his bags and got ready. Then, they had breakfast.

All the while, he was having the pendant in his hand. Suddenly, Periyachi noticed it and asked Shenba where he found it. Shenba said he found it in the back house. He asked her whether she knew anything about it.

She said she knew nothing much, but it was similar to the one her father-in-law wore in those days. It was given to him by Tharanga Rajan's grandfather who happened to be the village chief in those days. Shenba enquired was there a possibility that both were the same. She said it couldn't be.

Because the pendant worn by her father-in-law was buried along with him. He died even before Chandrakumar was born. Shenba asked the reason for Tharanga Rajan's grandfather giving that pendant to Chandrakumar's grandfather.

Periyachi didn't know anything more than that. Shenba enquired about her father-in-law's burial ground. She said her father-in-law was buried near the forest border. Shenba looked closely around the pendant and also smelled it.

It was made up of a brass tiger headed figure with fine carvings of the tiger face. The head was tied with the teeth of an animal, probably a tiger on both sides. The whole rope was made of human hair and animal hair. The pendant reeked with the smell of blood.

Shenba finished his breakfast and went to his room to bring up the luggage. Gunalini brought some lemons and camphor on a plate with some water. Periyachi burned the camphor and looped the ceremonial plate thrice in front of Shenba's face.

Then, she did the same with the lemon and then threw the pieces of lemon in various directions. She then told Shenba the evil spirits and eyes had been waded off, now he could go.

Chandrakumar started his bike. A servant carried the luggage to the bike. After bidding adieu to everyone, Shenba left their home with Chandrakumar towards the bus stop. While crossing the village, everyone stared at Shenba which made him realize that they knew the reason for his arrival.

3

MISSING FRIEND

After a fairly long ride on the bike, they arrived at the bus stop. Chandrakumar went to enquire about the bus from the vendors nearby. Something struck Shenba's mind, and he stood frozen for a while, as if recalling memories from the past. Then suddenly, he flapped open his bag and went through various books and articles that he got from the central library.

Amidst them was a folded paper, old, crumbled on the edges and yellowish in colour from the layer of oxidised lignin. A smile flashed over his lips as he realized the paper was nothing, but a map of the surrounding forests scaled by the local officials.

Chandrakumar returned, informing the bus would arrive within a few minutes.

"Where did you get this from?" He looked at the piece of paper.

"It's a map, drawn by the locals. Found it in the book I got a while ago from the library, when I was studying about Parangikadu."

Chandrakumar scratched his head, trying to cope up with

Shenba's excitement.

"Hold this. Will you?"

Chandrakumar grabbed the map from Shenba as he took out the map drawn by the reporter.

"Look!" Chandrakumar exclaimed. "According to this map the forest is stretched to 2.8 miles to be exact. And I guess this is the lake from that map."

Since the forest was intact, it was pronounced reserved even though people travel through it. Shenba was not worried to know that the area was deprived from network signals as he never owned a cell phone. His unique style of living has always made him stand away from the crowd. The map was detailed enough to spot the water bodies and mountains. Chandrakumar, pointed to another lake in the forest which, to his surprise, he had never seen before. Then he consoled himself as he said to Shenba that the lake was totally on the opposite side of the path they took and maybe that's why they might have not come across it.

The two lakes were the mirror images of each other, making Shenba curious about it. That bemused him more as he was not sure which lake was drawn by the reporter. While he was pondering over the map, the bus had already arrived. Shenba boarded the bus and bid farewell to Chandrakumar.

The bus moved from the bus stop. Shenba asked how much the fare was to reach Parangikadu to the conductor. Just as he was talking, the bus braked to a sudden halt.. All the eyes in the bus turned towards Shenba and the conductor. The conductor's shaking hands gave a ticket and said, "Twelve Rupees."

The bus again started moving. Until now songs were playing on the bus and there was constant chatter but now all had gone silent as if an apocalypse knocked the door.

The sun peeked through the mountain tops, a cold breeze

kissed the bare skin of Shenba's arms, making him shiver. The deep stare of the passengers gave Shenba goosebumps. The sounds of cattle intensified the pressure. Shenba silently took a book out on Parangikadu and started reading.

When he took his eyes away from the book and looked around, he found a few eyes turned away from him, pretending to be sightseeing. The bus conductor also looked keenly at him instead of counting his tickets. After some time, a small boy came towards Shenba, trying not to fall due to the constant jolting.

From under his book, Shenba could see a pair of legs near him. He closed the book and looked at the boy, hoping for an answer.

"What is it?"

"Papa." The boy said innocently. Shenba bewilderedly looked around. A passenger in his late 70's, told Shenba that the boy's father had been missing for the past two weeks.

"And his mother?"

"A few years ago the tigers got her. All that he has now is me. And all that I have is him. I am his grandfather."

"And why this special gaze at me?"

The old man smiled.

"Everybody Knows".

"Sorry?"

"I am Senrayan. I am a farmer. Mannaiyan is my son."

Shenba choked. The conductor tapped over Shenba's head to relieve the cough. Senrayan smiled again.

"He went missing?"

The man nodded, still smiling.

"And why are you smiling?"

"I see the light." He smiled at Shenba and then turned to the mountains.

The sun gleamed from behind it. When the sunlight fell on Shenba through the bus window, something started to glow inside Shenba's bag. It was the Tiger pendant.. He took it outside the bag. On seeing the pendant, everyone on the bus stood up from their seats and came near Shenba and touched his feet. Some women even started dancing wildly as if possessed by spiritual beings.

The whole world around Shenba was spinning too fast for him to realize or understand anything. And before he could say anything the bus came to a halt. Shenba stared in awe as the bus driver came to him, touched his feet and went back to drive the bus. Shenba turned towards Senrayan for answers, but he gestured to him to stop. He advised him to wear the pendant, and only then will he answer any questions.

Shenba wore the pendant around his neck. He felt something strange in his body as if a snake moved through his veins. For a moment, he couldn't even twitch his finger, frozen completely to his seat.. And then, he felt very powerful as his senses were heightened.

He could hear the driver's heartbeat while sitting in the back seat. His nose filled with the smell of bricks burning in a factory that was situated miles away! Even his eyesight got so intense that he could see the microbes in the air. Shenba now turned to Senrayan.

He started speaking as if he understood the mind of Shenba. Senrayan told that Rajan spoke highly about him in the village. That's how everyone knew about him. The whole village was waiting for his arrival as all of their other options had dried out.

Shenba asked where they were returning from.

"From Aiyanaar temple. It's in the outskirts of Puliyanur."

Shenba recalled the statue when he came with Chandra

Kumar. Senrayan told that it was God of protection for not only Puliyanur but also for Parangikadu.

People from the whole village offer something to God and pray for their safety. "And what is this pendant about?"

"Back when I was a child, I used to see a very few elders wear this pendant. Legend says, only those who wear it, can walk through the jungles safely alone. It was believed that **Puliyudaiyan** - a demigod who was half tiger and half-human, protected the people from tiger attacks. As ages passed, villagers opted for weapons for their safety and the belief vanished into thin air along with these pendants."

Shenba and other passengers were keenly listening to Senrayan, as he explained the history of their village and the tiger pendant. "And when did Mannaiyan go missing?"

"It has been two weeks."

Shenba was shaken to his core. "That... That's impossible. I saw him a day before. In fact, he came with Rajan's letter!"

The public gasped. "Show it to me." Senrayan asked for the letter. Shenba handed it to him just to be left in shock.

"It's a blank paper son." Senrayan waved the blank piece of paper in the air. A startled Shenba started fumbling through his belongings. He suddenly took out the map drawn by the reporter, which to his surprise, was also blank. Senrayan smiled and asked what was written in the letter carried by Mannaiyan. Shenba told Senrayan that it was a letter from his friend Tharanga Rajan asking him to come over to the village to solve the mystery.

He started to laugh very loudly. His laughter could be heard even from a mile away. The more curious conductor asked the reason for Senrayan's laughter. But nothing got past his ears. Shenba and the Conductor looked at each other in puzzlement. They thought that Senrayan had gone mad due to the missing of his son.

Shenba again asked Senrayan to stop laughing and reason with them. "My dear son. Tharanga Rajan was the first person who went missing! So now you tell me how can a missing person send a letter through another missing person?!"

Shenba now realizing that his friend is missing as well felt guilty for not being around him when he needed him the most.

Shenba asked Senrayan how they knew so much about him if Tharanga Rajan was already missing. Senrayan told Shenba that Tharanga Rajan was talking about Shenba right from the day when Indrakumar got lost.

His decision to call upon Shenba was opposed by Sureya, a soothsayer. The people of the village were superstitious which in turn made them accept and follow Sureya blindly. As everyone on the bus was listening to Senrayan, there was a loud noise and trembling on the bus. The bus stopped rashly.

Everyone hurt themselves knocking their limbs here and there. Shenba and the conductor walked to the front. The driver got down from the bus to inspect.

Then, he told everyone to get down from the bus. Shenba enquired the reason. The driver replied the bus broke down. It would take hours to repair it. So, the people had no other way except to walk. All the passengers took their luggage and started to walk.

Shenba took his bag and got down from the bus. The conductor came near Shenba and wished him good luck. Shenba nodded thankfully. Suddenly, someone held Shenba's hands. Shenba turned and found the boy was holding his hands.

Now, Shenba gave some chocolates that he had in his pockets. Shenba asked the boy what was his name. "Puliyan." The boy replied.

Senrayan said that the boy was named in remembrance of the Puliyudaiyan god. Shenba asked how long it will take to reach the village.

"Half a mile I would say." Someone started singing a folk song, to which Senrayan said, "They sing it to gain strength and also to keep any tigers at bay. The folk song was about the Puliyudaiyan god and the density and beauty of the forest. Many passengers took turns to sing.

4

THE WITCH'S ENTRY

O Puliyudaiyan, please protect us!
For thou art righteous;
Thy kingdom ranker aught more!
We people from thine aery,
Amerce those who berattle thee;
Thy blazon bruits in jungle!
The blood civet of thy enemies' corses,
Wonder-wound flowers civet!!
Chaps of tigers tremble in fear of thyself
To which we pray thee!
O Puliyudaiyan, please protect us!

As he was immensely listening to the song, Shenba didn't hear Senrayan calling him. Senrayan shook the shoulders of Shenba. Suddenly, Shenba realized and came back to his senses. He just smiled and told him the song was nice. Then, Senrayan pointed towards the mountains. A beam of light shone straight from the land to the skies, as if an unearthly signal to a world beyond.

"What on earth is that Senrayan?" Shenba asked.

"The pillar of light appeared since the first person went missing. The villagers believe that the souls of every person that went missing are being sent to the world beyond ours. The transmission could not be interrupted at any cost, so all the tigers went away to protect it."

"And do you believe it?"

"Well there's no proof to it. But belief is what binds us villagers together, whether it be the souls flying away or the prayers we chant for our safety.

Shenba nodded smilingly. He looked at the light. There was some kind of movement up and down the beam. And then he was shocked as a tiger faced human figure flashed within it.

"Senrayan look! The Human Tiger!"

Senrayan laughed. "Just remove the pendant Shenba. And you will be fine. He removed the pendant and realized that he can hardly picture the light.

Senrayan said that was the power of the pendant. When Shenba asked about the shape he saw in the light to Senrayan, he didn't reply. Now, Shenba recalled the reporter saying something about the TIGER PEOPLE.

He wondered out loud, "Could it be one of them?!" As they were moving on, Shenba noticed some movement in the mountain. He wore the pendant again and looked towards the mountain. He spotted a tiger moving swiftly parallel to the passengers.

"Ok. So there's a tiger walking right beside us Senrayan. It's hidden in the bushes."

"They don't attack people in group Shenba."

And then the tiger roared. Shenba felt a hand grab around his. It was Puliyan. He was scared enough to let go off Shenba's hand.

"Look." Senrayan pointed at the road ahead. A signboard stood damaged at the edge of the road, covered in thorns and bushes.

As they almost reached the village, The sun started to disappear behind the thick branches of the trees and soon there was hardly any sunlight around. Even if it was the middle of the day, it seemed as if the sun was about to set.

A few huts scattered around filled the barren lands of the village area. As Shenba went further, there stood a big bamboo statue of tiger and human blended figure—Puliyudaiyan. Everyone prayed before him for a few minutes, thanking him for bringing them safely to their homes. Then, everyone started to disperse. Shenba started to walk away, when a human skull fell down and came rolling right under his feet.

Everyone, including Shenba, were shocked to witness it. He looked around anxiously just to notice an old lady staring at Shenba angrily. She held onto a staff with a tiger head. Her hair coiled over her head into what appeared to be a crown decorated with Rudraksha beads. She wore a big, beautiful nose ring made of gold strings that ran all the way up to her lobe and sat at the bottom of her earring. Her body is marked with tattoos, stretching from neck to toes and she muttered something angrily under her breath.

Shenba knew the moment he saw her, that the woman was none other than Sureya. And then she finally spoke. "Go Back", she shouted. "You've brought this village a curse that will bring nothing but destruction. Wherever you go, death will follow. And wherever you stop, darkness will spread!"

Shenba bent down patiently and picked up the skull.

Dusting it properly, he handed it back to Sureya and walked away without uttering a word. But Sureya was not finished yet. She blocked Shenba's path again, holding the staff in front of him. Shenba grabbed the staff and all of a sudden a lightning struck over the staff throwing both Shenba and Sureya apart. Fear startled those who witnessed the moment. Shenba got up and dusted his clothes. To his surprise, both the staff and the pendant were glowing now. He picked up the staff. Nothing happened. His eyes widened as he noticed Sureya was wearing a pendant as well.

She, unaware of Shenba's surprised expressions, got up and chanted some mantras. As she picked up ash from a pit nearby, she enchanted some more, and then walked away spreading the ash without even claiming the staff. Shenba started to walk into the village, with the staff still in his hands and Senrayan walking beside him. As they walked, the wind started to blow faster, and dust devils formed all around. The clear sky filled up with dark clouds, and it became harder for the people to even walk. But none of these bothered Shenba. He walked as if it were one of his morning strolls. Puliyan held onto Shenba's hand in fear. Senrayan shook Shenba to which he just turned and smiled.

He was baffled by his gestures. That is when he noticed Shenba's eyes glistening like a star. The path to the village was a mud road, covered with thorny bushes on both sides in a manner to prevent wild animals from crossing across the road. After a few minutes' walk, they entered the main village.

The houses in the village were not built in an orderly manner. All the houses were scattered here and there. Apart from the strange order of houses, the village appeared to be suffering from a severe famine. Some houses were too ruined to live in and seemed to be left abandoned for a long period. Suddenly, Puliyan left hold of Shenba's hands and ran into a hut. He came out with a photo album and handed it over to Shenba.

He looked at the photograph. It was the family photo of the Senrayan family. An old lady came up to Shenba. Her back bent into a crooked shape, and her wrinkles hung down the cheeks.

She laid her cold fingers over Shenba's face and muttered something. As she walked away, Senrayan took away his bag and placed it aside. Without knowing how to react to the weird hospitality, Shenba again started looking at the photograph. Four people stood smiling in the photograph, among which Shenba pointed at a woman and asked, "Who's she?" Senrayan bent his head as if grieving. "That's my daughter in law, Maadammal."

"What happened Senrayan?"

And before he could answer, a tiger leaped out of the bushes and dug his claws deep in Senrayan's back. He tried to get away, but before he could run for it, the tiger sunk his deep teeth into Senrayan's soft flesh, killing him instantly.

5

MYSTERY AND HISTORY OF THE PALACE

Silence followed the happening. The tiger disappeared back into the bushes, leaving everyone stunned with fear.

Puliyan started to scream in pain and agony. He ran towards his dead grandfather, but Shenba pulled him away and held onto him tightly, fighting Puliyan's constant subconscious struggles. Shenba wanted to tear himself apart, but he kept himself together somehow.

All the villagers gathered around the dead Senrayan. The roaring of the people was evident for Senrayan's dignity and respect among the people of Parangikadu. Few men among the crowd lifted Senrayan's corpse and placed it in front of his house. Puliyan placed a tiger doll at the feet of Senrayan's corpse. He told Shenba wailing that it was made by his grandfather for his last year's birthday. As time started passing, more crowds started gathering around the place.

Clouds hid the sun and darkness followed a figure that approached Shenba. It was Sureya.

"You!" She exclaimed angrily. "You brought death and destruction to this village! Senrayan's death was just the beginning of what is about to come!". Shenba didn't utter a word. But then, a few villagers shouted from among the crowd, "Go away!"

"No! He's the messiah! Did you forget what happened on the bus!" A few others shouted in his support.

Mild chaos started to arise over Senrayan's corpse. Puliyan was too saddened to notice or understand anything. The situation escalated as villagers started pushing each other. That was enough for Shenba.

"STOP!!" He shouted and stomped the staff of Sureya on the ground. The stomping shook the ground which made everyone quiver. Shenba's eyes gleamed as he looked at the villagers with rage. The staff and the pendant glowed bright. "Leave." He roared. Within a few moments, the crowd vanished. Sureya ran away as if being chased by a beast. Shenba slowly calmed down.

The old lady brought food for him and placed it at his feet as if he was a God who reincarnated. "Tell me everything."

"My name is Battammal. I'm 99 years old." She continued, "The disappearances in the village are my doing." And she started crying. People gathered around again hearing the cries of the old lady.

Shenba was taken aback by those words. He consoled her and told her to continue. "There is a palace inside the jungle." Shenba recalled the reporter saying something similar.

Battamal continued, "The palace is the residing place for the Tiger People's King, Puliyudaiyan., who ruled these lands when the Tiger People lived here, in the Dhüvabära Yuga."

"As the yuga cycle changed to Kali Yuga, their people either died or changed into present-day tigers."

"How do they look?" asked a child.

"They are mostly minor shape-shifters. But their true form is the Head and limbs of a tiger, and a body quite humane, along with a tail. This gave them the hunting ability of a tiger and intelligence of a human. They can shapeshift between a full tiger and fully human for a short period."

"So, there were humans when they were present?" asked another child. Battamal nodded. "Though they were civilized then, as they started to evolve, they became mindless beasts, as they are today," told Battamal.

"At the beginning of Kali Yuga, the Tiger people were living peacefully with humankind among various kinds. But, as Hindu Mythology states the good deeds were one-fourth and the bad deeds were three-fourth in Kali Yuga. The humans got greedy and started to destroy forests and kill anyone/anything who stood in their way. The changing of the forest environment was one of the primary causes for the Tiger people to evolve into these beasts," she continued.

"The Tiger people and the Humans started attacking each other. The humans were more in number which paved the path of destruction for the Tiger people." Puliyudaiyan, the King of Tiger People, worried about the safety of his people. As he was a great magician, he put a powerful spell over his people and his palace to hide them away from humans. But at the same time, he was also worried about breaking the bond between humans and his kind."

"Hence, he imbued some powers over certain objects. The person who possesses the object would be considered as an ally of Tiger people and will be protected from tiger attacks," Battamal concluded.

She pointed to the pendant, "It's one of those objects." "But how are you responsible for the deaths and the missings?"

"The magic that makes the palace invisible to the human eye

has a strong connection with the offerings the tigers make. It is believed that the tigers hunt to provide food for the king and his people.

"The tigers place the offerings and clear the place, because when the king comes down, no soul should be wandering around. That could weaken the magical force that separates their world from ours.

"But one day, I was returning home with Maadammal, and due to my weakness I sat by the lake to drink some water. Maadammal offered me some food she found near the lake to make me feel better. What we didn't know was that it was an offering made by the tigers to the Tiger People.

"When the barriers opened, Maadammal was drawn to the gates like an insect is drawn to light. I tried to stop her but was too weak to do anything. Before I could think of anything I fainted."

"The next morning, passersby helped me up and took me to the village. No one believed me back then when I told them the story. For once, even I thought I had lost it. But then I realized Maadammal was gone for real, and everyone was too ignorant to believe the cause." She broke into tears again. The villagers consoled her and requested Shenba not to ask anything else from her.

A lot of questions popped up in Shenba's head, more like dots that he needed to connect to get a clear picture. With all those thoughts in his mind, he couldn't realize when he fell asleep. When he woke up the next morning, birds chirped around him and he could even hear a few villagers gossiping around. Shenba looked around while getting up. The photo album was right over him. He took it and placed it aside. As he yawned something abruptly struck his mind. He turned back to the photo frame and picked it up again, taking a good look at it.

He spotted some tattoos on Maadammal's hands. He knew they were familiar. "Got it! Sureya had them! And so did the reporter! But that could possibly mean only one thing. They all have visited the palace!

6

FOUND EVIDENCE AND UNFOUND PEOPLE

Shenba jumped with shock and wanted to know about the tattoos. The two of three people who had tattoos had already visited the palace. But that might also mean that Sureya had also visited the palace, though how she returned sane, is yet to be found.

Shenba left for sight-seeing once he finished his morning chores. Puliyan and a few other children accompanied him. Shenba still had the staff and the pendant with him, as if it were his new alliance. The village was more of a forest than any usual and appropriate human habitat. The people of the village mainly depended on the goods they availed from the forest and the goods obtained from trading with nearby villages.

Farming was not the main business, as it was in Puliyanur. As the name suggests, the village was mainly full of rocks and dense trees. While wandering in the village, the children took Shenba near a long rock-like structure. It was an ancient monolith, with some foreign language engraved in it. When Shenba went near the monolith, the carvings on that started to glow.

The children started to shout in wonder. Shenba understood that the glowing was something related to the staff. "I have seen this before, when Sureya came by it!" A child exclaimed.

Shenba smiled to himself realising his assumption was correct. "Do you care to elaborate?"

The boy told Shenba that he was returning to the village after grazing the animals. Suddenly, he saw Sureya was doing some chanting near the monolith. "I hid nearby in some bushes, hoping to see some forbidden magic. That is when the monolith glowed. Sureya made it glow."

Shenba asked the boy why he had not told this to anybody. The boy replied it was due to Maadammal. She also saw the glowing that day. When she saw the boy, she asked him not to tell anybody. "I decided to ignore her warnings and tell everyone anyway. But then I was taken aback when the very next day Maadammal went missing. I thought if I said it to anyone, I would be gone too. But I don't want to!"

"And was Maadammal bearing any tattoos?"

"No. None."

Shenba pondered over questions intensely. But the children were not ready to hang around anymore. "Let's get out of here." One of them suggested.

"But I want to read these engravings." Shenba insisted.

It was something ancient. At first, he assumed it was written in Greek but, after thorough viewing, he found it was ancient Tamil.

Though Shenba found it difficult to translate the language, he translated with the help of a picture shared by his friend from a museum. Interestingly, the monolith confirmed the presence of the Tiger Palace.

It also described in detail about the treasures and artifacts present in it. A few important magical rituals were also noted in bold underneath the script that had to be performed to enter the palace. After absorbing this information, Shenba got back to the village with the children. Shenba was making notes of whatever he found and heard that day. A quick question popped into his mind out of the blue.

If Maadammal didn't have the tattoo on her body, then when was the photo of her hands with the same tattoo taken? Who took this picture and why?

Shenba was curious and wanted to find the answer to it all. At first, he thought of asking Battammal, but then again, he didn't want to disturb her as she was ill. These questions would only add up to her weakness.

Considering he had no other choice, he went on by himself to find his answers. He went to Tharanga Rajan's house, opened the door and entered. Everything was shabby yet from Shenba's point of view, it was cleaner than his own house. A photo of an old couple hung on the wall with a garland over it. "Must be his parents." He murmured to himself.

And then he found a photo of himself with Tharanga Rajan. His nostalgic memories were interfered when he heard a crashing noise in the very next room. A boy was leaning over the high window frame, about to take his life. Shenba, impulsively, jumped towards him to save him but the boy escaped. He disappeared into the darkness "What was he here for?" Shenba questioned himself loudly as he searched for clues around him. That's when he found a set of sheets scattered near a large leatherbound briefcase. When he examined them closely. He saw that those papers were various journal entries and reports made by the reporter. Among this mess, there was an unfinished sheet that contained details about the disappearances in the village.

Shenba then opened the briefcase. It happened to be the

briefcase of that same reporter. "I am not the first person that Tharanga Rajan had contacted!" Shenba thought to himself.

He searched the briefcase for further clues. He found an identity card that belonged to the reporter. His name was Amuthavanan.

Then, Shenba read the notes of the reporter. In his notes, Amuthavanan had made entries explaining the first day of his visit to the village. He was on the verge of solving the mystery of the village before he had turned mentally ill.

When Shenba went on to close the briefcase, he found the reporter's full-size photograph. He was surprised to discover that even the reporter also had no tattoos on his hand. Then, Shenba deduced that the only person who could answer this puzzle was Sureya.

But Shenba wanted more concrete evidence before confronting her. So, he wanted to check up on the police report. Chandrakumar had given him his contact, and now it was the right time for Shenba to contact him. He asked Chandrakumar to bring all the details and evidence collected by the police regarding that case.

After a few long hours, Chandrakumar along with the Inspector of Police came to Parangikadu. The Inspector handed over the files to Shenba who thoroughly went through every detail of the report.

Chandrakumar spread a white cloth on the floor and started to organise the evidence for Shenba to inspect. He made sure nothing got tampered. The police report in the hands of Shenba read as follows:

- All the disappeared people are assumed to be killed, as all of them got lost in the middle of a dense jungle where tiger sightings are frequent.

- No concrete evidence was found during the investigation for explaining the phenomena of disappearance.
- A torn cloth with some bloodstains was found amidst the jungle which belonged to Indrakumar. This was confirmed by Indrakumar's brother, Chandrakumar.
- A few tiger teeth and claw nails were found, and a few paw marks supported the evidence.
- A pocket diary was acquired from a mentally unstable reporter who was found wandering in the jungle. This evidence was discarded as it had only personal information about the reporter and his daily deeds.

Shenba enquired about the diary. The Inspector said that they got it from the reporter's pocket when they were treating him for his illness. Shenba got the diary and read it.

11.10.2018 – I got the letter from Tharanga Rajan.

12.10.2018 – I reached Parangikadu.

13.10.2018 – Sureya was seen near the monolith.

14.10.2018 – I took a photograph of the Senrayan family and framed it by myself.

15.10.2018 – Senrayan's daughter in law went missing today. I and Tharanga Rajan went searching for her.

16.10.2018 – ....

The dairy was blank after the fifteenth of October.

"What happened then?" Shenba wondered.

7

MYSTERY UNFOLDS

Shenba flipped the pages again and again only to find it all empty. He asked the Inspector about any further details of the diary, but he replied, "Negative." Shenba's mind ran through the matter again and again trying to find any little detail that they might've missed. He examined tiger teeth and claw nails. They seemed to contain a few droplets of blood.

Shenba asked the Inspector whether they had checked those teeth and claw nails. He said that the forensic people had examined it already and found that the blood belonged to a human species. They couldn't find other details since the blood was old and very little. Shenba found that to be too convincing. He took out his materials and started to perform a ritual of dark magic by chanting a mantra for the first time in front of those people.

He told the Inspector that the magical spell will reveal the details about the blood. He pulled out a liquid and, while chanting, he poured it over the claw nails and teeth. The spots of red blood started to turn purple. Chandrakumar and

Inspector were in a state of shock to witness this kind of real magic for the first time in their life.

Shenba understood that this was not the blood of a human and explained that it is of an animal. The inspector was dumbstruck by the revelation. He asked Shenba to explain the phenomena of that discovery.

Shenba began to explain the process. “Each blood is the same. The only difference between the blood is the proteins that are used for self-identification. Those proteins not only vary between humans and animals but also between two human individuals. So, an antiserum is derived from an animal species and added to the blood sample. If the blood sample coagulates, then it would be human blood. The polymorphic potion derived by mixing various animal blood and human blood had the power to falsify the sample magically.”

Shenba also said that he added a dimorphic potion that nullifies the magic. If the blood on the nails and teeth were human, then, the stains on the evidence would be black. But now the stain was purple. So, Shenba concluded that the blood on the evidence was not of any human. So, there could be no way where that would belong to Indrakumar as the police had concluded.

The inspector still could not abridge the shocking revelation. Chandrakumar inquisitively asked what could have happened to Indrakumar and all other people who went missing.

Shenba said, “Only one person could answer that question, Sureya. Before that, I have some translation to do.”

Inspector said that he had enquired about Sureya already. He took out the statements that he had noted from Sureya and showed them to Shenba. The statement read as:

Dated on 18.10.2018

Witness Name: Sureya

1) What do you say about this incident?

These are the deeds of the god. These days, the younger generation doesn't bother to learn or follow anything about tradition or culture. Their misdeeds have angered the gods and brought this upon themselves and the whole village.

2) Where were you at the time of the incident?

I was out of town for a week on a spiritual journey.

3) What are these misdeeds? Is there anyone in particular that you are referring to as you speak?

They don't respect the elders and their ancestral beliefs. Tharanga Rajan and his friend Indrakumar are the persons I am talking about. They never respected the Puliyudaiyan God and always mocked those who worshipped him. So, the Almighty God has punished them. This is their fate.

Shenba pondered over sometime after reading the report. He seemed to get a clearer picture of what might have happened. Shenba pointing to the second statement in the witness report, he questioned the Inspector. He said they had verified it and concluded it was true.

Now, Shenba took Amuthavanan's diary and began reading out the notes. Inspector and Chandrakumar were confused, and they could not understand why Shenba was focusing on these scribbles.

Shenba pointed out that Amuthavanan had seen Sureya on 13.10.2018. The police statement was taken on 18.10.2018. So how could she have gone on a spiritual journey for a week?

Inspector said, "But she was not present in the village for a whole week. Nobody else saw her."

Shenba replied, "Yes, she was not present in the village, but it is a possibility that she never went on a spiritual journey either."

Chandrakumar, who couldn't control his zeal, asked, "Where do you think she was the whole time?" Shenba didn't respond.

"Maybe, the reporter might have marked his entry wrongly."

Shenba said, "Hmm. I strongly think this is not a mistake. I have another alibi who can confirm this note."

Inspector asked who the alibi was. Shenba pointed out the boy and told him that he had seen Maadammal with Sureya someday near the monolith.

Probably, it was the next day that Maadammal had gone missing. Inspector said there was a possibility that both days could be different even if what the boy had said was true.

Shenba flipped the pages to where some pictures lay loosely between the pages. Those were the pictures taken by Amuthavanan. He slipped them around and showed it to the Inspector. It was a picture of Tharanga Rajan and Amuthavanan. The other one was a picture of Mannaiyan and his wife Maadammal. They examined the pictures closely. Both the photographs were dated 12.10.2018 which was hand-written by Amuthavanan. It was the same day he had arrived at Parangikadu.

Shenba turned towards the photograph of Senrayan's family that hung on the wall in a thick frame. In that photograph, Maadammal bore a tattoo on her hand, but she didn't have any on her hand in the first photo.

Right then, it hit them. Shenba asked Chandrakumar if he had seen the same tattoo elsewhere.

Chandrakumar recollected his memories and replied, "On the reporter's hands." Shenba said that he had also seen the same tattoo on Sureya's hands.

All three of them went to see Sureya in her house. Her house was on the outskirts of Parangikadu. When they reached the house, it seemed to be in a mess. It looked as if the building had deserted for many days.

The Inspector and Chandrakumar were perplexed. Shenba stood quietly, without a stutter. He asked both of them to step away from the house. He then performed some chanting which created whirlwinds around the house.

To their surprise, the house suddenly turned out to look clean and quite new. They entered and began rummaging every place possible. They searched every corner in the house for some kind of a clue. If there was one thing that Shenba was clear about, it was the fact that Sureya was a powerful witch.

The Inspector and Chandrakumar searched for the physical clues and Shenba searched the house for mystical evidence. In about an hour, the Inspector found animal heads stacked behind a long cupboard and stains of blood on them. Meanwhile, Chandrakumar found some tattoo ink on one of the shelves in the kitchen.

A secret lair inside the house had come to Shenba's notice. He figured it was magically bound. It was hard at first, but he managed to break the spell. When he did, it opened wide and all of them entered. They were surprised that such a large place was hidden inside an average sized house. They wandered around, letting it all sink in. Each of them spread out in different directions to investigate and inspect the place. It seemed as if it was impossible to search the entire place with just 3 pairs of eyes. Fortunately, in a short span of their arrival into the lair, they found a long string of exotic shining materials in the lair. It was more like a treasure hoard.

Shenba examined the materials. He said that it seemed to be exactly like those from the Tiger Palace. The Inspector and Chandrakumar found this extremely hard to believe. How was that possible? He took out some notes that he had translated before and showed it to them. He explained what was written in it and said they were writings engraved on the monolith in the village. Suddenly, a cough sound echoed.

Everybody turned in the direction from where the sound seemed to have come. It was so dark that they couldn't see even if there was something as close as 10ft from where they were standing. They moved quietly and carefully in an orderly fashion. To their surprise, a boy was lying on the ground in a semi-conscious state.

His shirt was torn in a few places as if he was stuck in a thorn bush. His left leg was swollen, and he was holding a bag in his hands. Shenba recognized him to be the same boy who jumped out of the window from Tharanga Rajan's house when he was there. The Inspector's jaw instantly dropped when he heard this.

Chandrakumar lifted the boy and patted his cheeks to wake him. When he didn't respond, he rubbed under his feet rapidly. Shenba took a serum from his pocket and put it in the boy's mouth. In a few moments, he coughed up some puke and opened his eyes. He had regained his consciousness but only partially. The Inspector began questioning him. The boy was a resident of Parangikadu.

The boy spoke, "Sureya drugged me so she could steal some documents that belonged to the reporter from Tharanga Rajan's house through me. As soon as I knew someone was there, I jumped out of the window by not just taking the document but the whole bag."

Meanwhile, Chandrakumar searched for the bag. The boy had sprained his leg and had gotten his clothes stuck in thorns while jumping from the window. When he had reached the spot, no one was there. Because of weakness from all the running the boy had fainted here.

Shenba explained that it was the effects of the drug. He gave him an antiserum which was why he puked, although the tiredness would remain for a while.

"Proper rest and some food should bring his health back." said Shenba. They now examined the bag. The bag contained many documents on Parangikadu. The bits and pieces of the story seemed to slowly fall in place. Among these documents, there was a sheet that explained how the mystics of Tiger Palace in the village could be put to an end. Shenba read each line carefully. He concluded that Sureya had definitely gone to the Tiger Palace.

He asked Chandrakumar to take the boy to the village and stay with him. Inspector and Shenba moved towards the forest from there.

It all seemed okay when they began their journey, but along the way, it got harder. The roads became steep, crowded by bushes and thorns. Insects and ugly little creatures wandered about the edges, sometimes creeping over their feet. They shrugged it off since some parts of the forest are not that beautiful but after a while, it began to get dark, pungent, and creepy. It seemed like it was a deep dark cave.

The natural light slowly disappeared, and they had to use their torch. This added more terror to the environment. After a tiresome hour, they reached the other end of the cave.

To their surprise, they were led back in the forest but this time it was at the bottom of a majestic mountain. Chandrakumar and Inspector were both astonished by the magnificence of the forest.

The full moon added beauty to the tall trees and made the water puddles here and there glitter. When they turned back, they noticed that a tiger's head covered the side of the entrance they had just come from. The sounds of owls hooting could be heard. But as far as they could see, only thorny bushes and dark trees were visible.

The Inspector asked Shenba where they should go next and what they should do to proceed further. Shenba took the notes and searched for any kind of clues. Among them there was a riddle:

To find what none can see;
Reach the top of one tree;
To enter the gates free;
Beware to become a wee.

The Inspector looked towards Shenba to solve the riddle. Shenba told the Inspector that the words "*none can see*" may denote the palace. So, Inspector asked whether they should start climbing a tree as it read "*Reach the top*".

Shenba said it would not be that easy. He pointed out the fact that it was mentioned to be one tree, not any tree. He looked around the cave for markings regarding the riddle. There were some stone carvings about how early people worshipped the gods and entered the temple.

Shenba suddenly took the Tiger pendant from his pocket and wore it. He gave the staff to the Inspector. Now, to their surprise, they could see a trail of the magical line pointing them a path. Without any further delay, Shenba started to follow the trail. Inspector tailed Shenba into the deep dark bushes of the forest.

8

THE TIGER TRAP

After a long walk into the deep forest, they stopped for a few minutes of rest. Suddenly, they felt some foul smell as if a corpse was decaying. Both of them searched around. In a dark bush, they found a decaying corpse of a deer.

Shenba told the Inspector that they were nearing the Palace. Without further delay, they again started to follow the trail. Half an hour passed; they reached a plain area where the trail ended. Shenba looked around for any further clues.

Inspector also searched for evidence around. Abruptly, the Inspector called Shenba in a loud voice. Shenba rushed towards him. Inspector showed him some footprints of a tiger. Shenba looked around. The place was surrounded by tall trees which appear to be the same in all ways.

Shenba also noticed that their footprints started to vanish as they moved on. Inspector was terrified. Because they now lost the path they came through. Now both of them had no idea of how to escape the place.

Shenba took a moment of silence and tried to recall everything as possible as he could. Then, he remembered about the riddle. Shenba told the Inspector to search the trees for any kind of weirdness. They both scattered and searched again for any kind of clues.

All the trees had the claw marks of tiger and some blood here and there over them except one. Shenba inspected the tree carefully and concluded that it was not a tree at all.

It was a stone structure that appeared to be in the form of a tree. Shenba told the Inspector that it was the ONE TREE. Inspector was puzzled and enquired Shenba about his conclusion. Shenba told about his deductions as follows:

- All the trees had claw marks and blood over them because tigers would climb and rest over them.
- But this tree had none because the tigers couldn't climb due to their CAT type climbing ability.
- The tree was so steep that it had to be climbed like a MONKEY or HUMAN in our case.
- That tree was not a real one which makes the tigers avoid that.
- Last but not least, this button couldn't be reached by the tigers.

By saying that Shenba pressed a button on the stone tree. The next moment, a series of ladder-like steps came out of the stone tree through the top. Inspector was awestruck by seeing this.

Shenba started to climb the tree and reached the top. He could see almost every part of the jungle in all directions. He could see the lake mentioned on the map. But to his disappointment, he couldn't find the palace. Then, he remembered that he removed the tiger pendant when they reached that place. He took it out of his pocket and wore it.

Again, he looked around. There it was. A huge glittering palace fully made up of gold, diamonds, rubies, emeralds, etc. Shenba was mesmerized by its beauty.

A flash of wind made him regain his consciousness. Suddenly, he found something was moving among the trees. He concluded that those were tigers. He shouted to alert the Inspector, but everything went in vain. He took a step forward and shouted again.

When he took the step, he pressed a button there unknowingly. This button made all those steps to retract inside the stone tree. So, Shenba jumped down by skipping many steps like a mountaineer. When all the steps retracted, Shenba had no other go than to fall. Shenba fell with a loud noise. Inspector lifted him. They both got ready for the tigers in defensive mode.

Both were looking in all directions around. With a roar, a tiger jumped in front of them. It was followed by three more. All the tigers surrounded them in a circular formation. They were in the middle of them. Inspector was in terror. A tiger jumped towards them. Both of them evaded sideways to avoid it.

The Inspector tried to shoot them with his gun. But the bullets could do no damage to them. Shenba told him that they were magical and only magic could completely defeat them. Then he threw some smoke bombs around them which gave them some time to plan something. Shenba then started some chanting. His eyes started to glow in green like an emerald. By this time, the smoke around them started to fade away in thin air. Now another tiger jumped towards him. Shenba used the staff while chanting. This created a magical current to pass through the staff and attack the tiger.

He used staff with similar magic towards the rest of the tigers. Now all the tigers had run away. Shenba came to his normal self. Inspector was holding a large stick as his weapon of choice. Now Shenba gave the Inspector a magical rope to tie around.

Inspector asked for the reason. Shenba told him that the rope might prevent him from any kind of magic created by the palace and things related to it.

Inspector questioned Shenba how Sureya could have gone past the tigers. "She didn't," said Shenba. Inspector was shocked to hear such a reply. "Then?" he questioned.

"She was the one who sent those tigers for attacking us," answered Shenba. The Inspector stood there for a moment in total shock. Shenba then told that the tigers won't attack the persons who held the magical objects like tiger pendant and the staff.

Sureya clouded the magic of these objects which made the tigers attack us. Inspector couldn't even fathom the fall of events. He got angry over Sureya for trying to kill them. They both rushed towards the palace. After a few skedaddling, they finally reached the lake. Nearer to the lake, the palace stood proudly with absolute beauty.

The palace was so huge that it completely covered the entire mountain behind it. The full palace was made of gold which made the place so bright as if a large bonfire was lit. The entrance of the palace was sided by two golden tiger statues. The eyes of the tigers were made up of Emerald.

Before the entrance, there were four-story inward fountains. Above it, there was a huge statue of Puliyudaiyan. There were guards all around the palace. Each guard was half tiger and half-human. All of them were a minimum of seven feet high. They wore metal cloth around their waist. Each carried a spear and shield with a tiger face on it. The palace was a six floored building. The length and breadth of the palace were around Two hundred feet long. The height of the palace was around One hundred and fifty feet high. The rooms of the palace were around One Thousand in number. The reflection of the palace was not visible in the lake. The windows were made up of

Oaktree as they were the favourite for tigers. The door of the entrance was made up of Sandalwood and stood Ten feet high. Songs of amusement could be heard in the palace. There were firecrackers visible in the sky. But none of them were reflected in the lake. Then suddenly everything stopped.

Instruments were playing in an orderly fashion indicating a King's entry. Suddenly a flying cart appeared in the sky. It was in a smoke form indicating that it was not physical. The moment the cart entered the palace gates it attained a physical form. The cart door slowly opened. A leg came out and landed on the footrest.

9

KING'S ENTRY AND WITCH'S HISTORY

Shenba and the Inspector were watching keenly. Drums were beating in a rhythm, rapidly - preparing for the big welcome. Now, they both noticed that it was not a human leg but of a tiger. As the curtains in the cart moved, a large person (or thing) appeared. Right at the moment, Shenba concluded that it was the Tiger King, the one and only, Puliydaiyan.

The tales and songs were never bluffing about his enormity and manliness. He was taller than all the tiger people. He had a broad chest that was twice the size of two people's. His arms had large biceps that looked strong enough for one to tie a rope and swing on it. He wore boots made of gold that retained his magnanimity and supremeness of wealth. After seeing him, the room was filled with sounds of music and joy. There were firecrackers twice the amount than earlier.

Even some of the tiger women blushed while welcoming their king with Aaradhanai (Homage/Worship with camphor). A few moments later, Puliyudaiyan entered the place in a royal fashion surrounded by his guards and people. Even the guards who were at the gate had followed him inside the palace.

Now, Shenba told the Inspector that this was their cue to enter the palace. They both hurried quickly. When they tried entering the gate, they were bounced off as if they were thrown away by someone. This caused a mystical rift in the magic around the palace which was sensed by the King. Shenba and Inspector got up from the ground. He knew he was in complete bewilderment which made him rub his head. Shenba now remembered the riddle. He then told the Inspector to lie down on his knees and crawl like a baby and He followed the same. To their amazement, they were inside the compound walls of the palace. By that time, the King had sent his guards all over the palace to tighten the security.

When Shenba looked up, the guards were nearing them. Despite Shenba's insistence, the Inspector tried to run away dropping the staff. The guards got hold of him and he tried to shout at the top of his lungs but even his ears couldn't hear his voice. The guards had the staff in their custody.

Now, Shenba had no other option rather than to follow the guards. While getting up, something strange came to his notice. A tattoo had appeared on his hand. This was the same tattoo on the hands of Sureya and others. He immediately rushed towards the guards only to see that they were dragging the Inspector into the backside of the palace. They went on and on until finally they came to a halt.

From there, they headed downstairs into a dark stingy dungeon. Shenba tried to follow but stopped when suddenly he heard the sound of someone's footsteps. He quickly moved towards the closest pillar and hid behind it. To his surprise, he found Sureya lurking in the shadows. When he tried to take a step forward, he found that the guards had returned. Shenba began to get anxious that something might've happened to the

Inspector. Hearing the guards, Sureya also hid behind a pillar. Shenba took advantage of the situation and made a move. He got hold of her, leaving Sureya terrified as she expected him to be a guard. After coming to her senses, she tried to evade him but Shenba was determined not to leave her. He asked her furiously about her actions. When Sureya didn't utter a word, Shenba questioned her again, this time more sternly.

After repeatedly questioning her, she said a few words that left Shenba confused. "Save them, Save them." she chanted again.

"Who should I save? The Inspector?" asked Shenba.

Sureya replied, "I didn't say 'him'. I said 'them'."

"Who are they?" shouted Shenba.

"All of them," said Sureya. Shenba couldn't understand what she was talking about. She began laughing hysterically and said, "Your friend and all others are alive."

Shenba was astonished to hear this. He couldn't even fathom the situation. Sureya continued, "You can either hold on to me and lose your friends forever or release me and I'll tell you more about where they are."

Shenba found himself in a biased situation. He agreed to let Sureya go but on one condition that she must keep her word and tell him everything she ever knew about his friends. Sureya nodded in agreement.

As soon as he let her go, Sureya straightened out her clothes and began narrating her side of the story. "I am Senrayan's daughter - the firstborn and Puliyan's biological mother. My real name is Soodammal."

Shenba was taken aback. He listened to her as she explained how two years ago, she and her husband had to pass through the forest while returning to their village from a marriage function. Halfway there, they lost their way. They heard a tiger's roar from a distance. Both of them sprinted towards the biggest tree. They could see a path between the thick grass and decided to go down it, believing it would get them out of there. As they reached the end of the path, they had come to an enormous lake and a big palace on the other side. They were absolutely dazed at the sight of the majestic building. Despite her refusal, Soodammal's husband took the offering made by the tigers and ate it.

By then, the palace guards came and arrested both of them. Confused and tongue tied, they didn't know what to do or say. They were then presented in the courtroom to their king. Both of them were terrified to see that the courtroom was filled with tiger people. Soodammal pleaded before the king but recently before their capture, the king had been informed of tiger killing along with the cubs by some humans. He was told that they were burned to death for the sole purpose of entertainment. This news had caused unrest amongst the tiger people. They wanted to punish and get their revenge. Hence, they all shouted in chorus, "Kill them, kill them!"

Hearing this, Soodammal cried louder, pleading for mercy for her husband's life. Her husband couldn't speak as he was bound by magic due to his eating of the offerings. This made him cry more and blow air through his mouth as if his mouth was shut with a piece of cloth.

Their plea for mercy and forgiveness went in vain because the protests of the crowd overpowered their cries. Puliyudaiyan stood up and walked towards Soodammal's husband. He drew his sword and swiftly pierced it through his chest. Soodammal was speechless. She couldn't watch her husband slowly succumb to death in front of her eyes. The courtroom filled with cheers and claps, but nothing reached her ears except the echo of her husband's cry. When the king came towards her, she begged for mercy again, but only for the sake of her only son, "Puliyan" who was named after His Highness, Puliyudaiyan.

This time, the king agreed to spare her and told Soodammal that she must suffer the fate of the tigers and their inability against humans due to poor memory. He then cursed her that she shall lose her youth and turn into an old lady. "You will lose your memory gradually and people who knew you will lose any memory they have of you as soon as you step out of the palace. You may only remember your son but eventually, that also will fade." With this curse upon her head, she was thrown out of the palace. The king then put a powerful magic field around the palace which could be entered only by the tigers and people who crawled with any magical artifacts.

Soodammal couldn't process everything that had happened. She couldn't move as if she was tied up. She could feel her skin shrinking to wrinkle and her shoulders slouching. She slowly walked with tears in her eyes towards the lake to quench her thirst. By step by step, inch by inch, she finally reached the lake. It was pitch dark as a thick blanket of clouds covered the moonlight. She drank the water from the lake. The clouds slowly cleared, and the moonlight reached the ground. Suddenly, Soodammal jumped in fright and shock.

The moonlight had made her face visible. She saw herself, old with tanned and wrinkled. She recognized that she had lost all her beauty. She appeared to be a completely different person to herself. She started to run in like a maniac around the lake. Soon, she was tired and hungry. She fell to the ground and started weeping. Suddenly, she heard some noises - noises of humans. She rose, filled with hope but then, she remembered that nobody would remember her. How would she explain her situation? What would they think of her? Not prepared for it all yet, she hid behind the bushes nearby. It was her father, Senrayan, who had come with a search party for her and her husband. She was tormented between the thoughts of going to the family and staying hidden forever as long as she might find some way to revert everything.

One among the search party found a piece of cloth with bloodstains on it and showed it to others. Finally, Soodammal decided to go to her family. When she tried to come out of the bush, she heard Senrayan telling others that the boy's mother was killed by the tigers and he and his son would adopt the kid as their own.

Soodammal was stunned to hear this. Why would someone adopt his grandchild as his grandchild again? she thought. She then remembered the curse that everyone would forget her. Traumatized by hearing those words she vowed to return to her child at any cost by retaining her old self. If not, she would take revenge on the Tiger King, Puliyudaiyan, and his people.

The next morning, she proceeded on her quest to reclaim her old self and her son. For about one full year, she met many mages, wizards, and witches but, neither any person nor any ritual could bring back her old life.

Soodammal was also gradually losing her memory and purpose. The love for her son had now turned into greed and agony for power. She slowly became dark. Sensing this she returned to Parangikadu with a new face and new identity as Sureya.

Without raising any suspicions, she carried out her plan to gain revenge. Sureya started to learn as much as she could about the palace and the tiger people. The more she learned, the more her greed increased. It was not only greed for wealth but also for magical power.

She used people to do her chores by magically binding them. After the chores were done, she would release them of their magic binding. But most of the time, the people were not relieved of their magic as the chores were often related to Tiger

Palace. The Palaces' magic affected all of them and made them behave like maniacs. Sureya used this opportunity and told the villagers that she would cure them with her powers.

She would tie the affected people in chains and study their behaviours and their causes. Slowly, she learned about the magical artifacts and started to use them. They cured most of the magic effectively. These events raised her to a demigod status amongst the villagers.

Very few questioned her activities. The important ones were Tharanga Rajan and Indrakumar as they were educated and asked for proof of everything. This created mild tension between them and Sureya.

Whenever an argument sparked, Tharanga Rajan would mention Shenba and his adventures. This was how the whole village came to know about Shenba Nagulan. It also prompted a secret rivalry between Shenba and Sureya. Sureya started using people as her lab rats and improvised her works. What followed was unexpected!

10

THE TIGER PRINCESS AND HER SOLUTION

Sureya was driven by her greed and anger, so she never thought of the consequences of her actions. The continuous influx of normal people into the tiger palace started causing a rift in the magic of the palace, causing the tigers to go awry.

Before this, events where people were killed by the tigers even when they were travelling alone were rare. But after Sureyas's puppets started to visit the palace, the tiger attacks became more frequent even when going with a crowd. Sometimes, the tigers started to visit the village and kidnap and kill the cattle and people alike.

One day, when Sureya was coming from the castle after her research to revert her magic, she saw Indrakumar coming in front of her. When he saw her, he approached her and tried to grab hold of the Olai Chuvadi (Palm Leaf Manuscript) in Sureya's hand.

Sensing the danger, Sureya cast a spell over Indrakumar and turned him into a mindless hobo. By that time she had gained proficiency in controlling tigers too. She summoned the tigers to drag him near the palace. That was how Indrakumar was captured in the palace.

The Tiger Summoning spell gave Sureya the perfect ruse, as any kind of police investigation would be futile, as it was closed as a 'tiger attack'.

After Indrakumar went missing, a reporter came to the village and started to enquire about things. Later it was said that Tharanga Rajan was the one who invited the reporter to write the article in the newspaper after he couldn't reach Shenba directly, hoping that he might visit the village after reading the article.

The reporter found out that Sureya was behind all those troubles and attacks. Before he could divulge anything to anyone, Sureya got control over him too. She was going to do the same thing to the reporter, as she did with Indrakumar, but she couldn't control the tigers as it was Amavasai (New Moon Day).

During that day, no normal magic could control the tigers as they would be at their worst wit and rage. So, she fled the scene to save her skin hoping that the reporter would be dead. She only came to know that the reporter was alive because Shenba had told the villagers about him. Sureya also confirmed Battammal's story about Maadammal and confessed that she was responsible for that as well.

The rage and greed in her turned her into a selfish lone predator somewhat similar to the tigers as per the curse. This made her attack her kith and kin. She held no memory of anyone or anything about her past. She concluded her story with heavy weeping.

Shenba felt pity for her, but questioned her again, "How do you remember everything now? Whatever you just said, was that the truth or are you trying to deceive us again?" Sureya promised Shenba that whatever she said was true to the core. The reason she remembered everything was the curse was valid only outside the palace whereas inside the palace the curse would be lifted.

Suddenly, she turned into a beautiful middle-aged woman. Shenba was taken aback by her beauty. Sureya alias Soodammal told him that every time she entered the palace, she found a great many ways to rectify her errors and even to revert her curse.

Yet, the moment she went out of the palace, she would become a completely different person driven by anger. She pleaded with Shenba to help her complete her quest. He doubted her purpose and became hesitant.

He still didn't believe her and suspected her to be acting. To make Shenba believe, Sureya revealed a major trap laid by her. Meanwhile, a loud thud and roar could be heard at the end of the hallway.

The sound came from the farthest corner of the hallway. Sureya told Shenba that her trap had started its motion. He became very uneasy and confused. Sureya told Shenba to follow her. She cast a powerful spell to make that night into a New Moon Night. It created an effect that made the tiger-people lose their minds and make them behave like savages.

As they were new to that complete tiger-ness, they even started to attack each other. To a single tiger, each and everyone was an enemy. Within a few minutes, there was a huge ruckus everywhere. The sounds of rattling and roaring echoed around the walls of the palace. By that time, Puliyudaiyan sensed the danger within his walls.

Since he was a powerful magician himself, he could resist the magic to some extent but at some point, he also gave in to the control of the spell. He started to groan in anger and pure savage rage. He drew his sword which was almost his height and started swinging it.

Whoever or whatever crossed his path was split into two halves. Sensing the imminent danger to everyone, Shenba shouted at Sureya, "How do we reverse the effects of this spell?" "Please help with my quest! It's the only way to reverse all this!" replied Sureya. "As if!" Shenba shot back at her, and pinned her to the wall in irritation.

Sureya explained, "There is an Olai Chuvadi that contains everything about the Tiger Palace's magic. It was given to the King by Lord Shiva as a token of their devotion in the previous Yuga. Completing this quest is the only solution to all of our current problems."

Shenba was still unsatisfied, but he gave in and said, "Don't even think of pulling any tricks, for that may be the last time you do so." Sureya nodded in agreement. "The Olai Chuvadi is in the King's prayer room. To reach it, we have to cross the hallway and go through the kitchen, then the dining hall, then the swimming pool, then the courtroom, and at last to the prayer room."

Shenba sighed. "That is a lot of rooms! Why do we need to cross these many?"

"The prayer room is on the far end of the palace."

They started their quest. They would only have moved a few meters ahead when they spotted two tigers rushing towards them from either side. Both of them stood in defensive positions. Sureya held the tiger as if it became a statue when it jumped towards her. Shenba levitated the tiger on the side to the other side and threw it over the other tiger.

Now both of them started to attack each other which cleared the path to the next room. It was the kitchen. It had four large furnaces each occupying a space of about twenty feet. Since the roof was high, each furnace with its outlet looked as if a large statue of a deity was placed around there. The furnace placements were in accordance with the directions.

All kinds of raw materials, both vegetarian and non-vegetarian were present. The half-human part made them eat vegetarian sometimes it seemed. Many raw materials were the offerings given by the tigers. The cutting tables were made at chest height.

Each cutting knife looked like a small sword and so sharp that even a slight swing with it would cut a large tree into half. When they were about to move, they noticed that a tiger entered the kitchen. Both of them hid behind a door. The tiger slowly moved step by step and jumped over one of the cutting tables. It started to squander on the raw food materials on the table.

It gobbled the food up as if it had been hungry for months. Suddenly a noise came from the next room. The tiger jumped towards the noise. It was a lady's voice screaming for help. Both Shenba and Sureya ran towards the voice. They got dumbstruck by the sight.

It was a storeroom. A tiger woman was screaming for help to save her skin. Two tigers were trying to attack her. She was fighting them so hard that she got scratched over her body by the tiger's paws and was bleeding. Shenba and Sureya were shocked to see her behave normally. Seeing both of them, she pleaded for help.

So, both of them took hold of each tiger and made them faint magically. Now, Shenba helped her and asked her about herself. The tiger woman told them that she was the daughter of Puliyudaiyan. Her name was Puliyavalli. That was the first time she came to the Tiger Palace.

Those many years, she was in another realm where she was

learning all kinds of tricks. Then Shenba asked why she couldn't get past those tigers. She told them that she was defending herself instead of attacking, because her skills prohibit her from using them against her people.

The reason why she didn't go savage was that Puliyudaiyan put a powerful guard spell over her before entering this realm. That was the reason she didn't change like others. She enquired about Shenba and Sureya. Shenba told her everything.

Puliyavalli told Shenba and Sureya that she would help them as it was a great regret for her father that he had killed Soodammal's husband as he always wanted peace between humans and tigers.

She swore that she would attain penance for her father's sins. She also told them to hurry up as the magic over her was fading and that she would also become savage within a few moments.

Now, Puliyavalli led the way and they both followed them. They crossed the dining hall. It was so large that it occupied a space of about two auditoriums. The dining table was placed in the midst.

The chairs around it were hundreds in number. There was a fifty feet portrait of Puliyudaiyan in the dining hall. All the plates and goblets were in gold. There was a nice aroma mixed with food and flowers which formed a unique combination in the dining hall.

They reached the swimming pool through a large doorway. They all got shaken by the sore sight there. There was blood everywhere. So many tiger parts were lying here and there. Some tigers were cut in half. The swimming pool was as long as the room itself which made it appear like a small lake. Water was being poured into the pool by crouching tiger statues on the corners of the swimming pool.

The blood got mixed with the water and made it look like a

blood lake. For a moment, Puliyavalli got a slight drowsiness and vomited. She couldn't stomach the sight of her people. Sureya's eyes clouded with tears as she saw the consequences of her actions.

Puliyavalli got up and urged them to move faster as they had less time. Because at that moment, the death toll was high, and there would be no way to revert everything to normal. So, they moved up faster. Now they had entered the courtroom. There was a twist for them there. Because they not only saw blood but also huge fire everywhere.

Every tiger was fighting with each other. It was more of a fight-break-fight. Puliyavalli told Shenba that the break indicated that they regained their senses and fight indicated mind control. This was random with every tiger. So no matter what, at least one tiger was always fighting. Puliyavalli then turned completely into a tiger.

She asked them to follow her tracks. Some tigers came to attack her whom she carefully evaded and led them into the burning fire. At one point she stood simply without moving and doing nothing.

11

MISSING PEOPLE FOUND

Sureya went near her to shake her. Suddenly, Puliyavalli jumped over her indicating that she became savage. Shenba was terrified at that sudden jump. Sureya thought she was dead and closed her eyes.

Shenba shouted, "Puliyavalli!" Now, Puliyavalli shook her head and moved away from Shenba. She told Shenba that she was more prone to mind control in the tiger form so they would have to hasten up.

Now Shenba conjured some magic and made her resist the mind control and told her that the spell would buy her some time. As they tried to move, a huge pillar crashed nearby them which made them scatter and fall on the floor.

A piece of the pillar fell over Puliyavalli which made her grievously wounded on the right hind-leg. Shenba and Sureya helped her to get up by moving the rubble. She could barely get up but she mustered her courage and strength and led them to the King's bedroom.

They got a glimpse of pure misery and hell. Puliyudaiyan was piercing his sword through the neck of a tiger while holding its head. Within a few seconds, the tiger was decapitated.

Puliyavalli shouted, "Your Highness!"

The King turned his head towards them and groaned in anger. Puliyavalli panicked, it seemed as if her father had also changed and become more savage due to his huge strength and magic.

She showed Shenba and Sureya the prayer room and told them that she would hold her father back. Shenba and Sureya rushed towards the prayer room to find Olai Chuvadi.

Puliyudaiyan swung his sword like a beast. Shenba and Sureya carefully evaded his swing. They entered the prayer room. It was a small room compared to all the other rooms in the palace. At the opposite end of the room, there was a Shivalinga statue.

The room had no torches for lighting. There was a long elliptical shape open on the roof. Below that opening, there was a crystal hanging. If one stands directly below it and looks up, it would resemble an eye.

The moonlight entered the room through that hole and fell on the crystal. The crystal scattered and refracted the light into the room in all directions possible which made the room brighter. To cap it all, the light scattered through all the objects in the room which were made up of gold, diamonds, rubies, etc.

That gave them a feeling that they had entered a treasure hoard. Without further impediment, both of them started searching for the *Olai Chuvadi* on each corner of the room.

Meanwhile, Puliyavalli was trying to knock some sense into her father by trying to converse with him. But all her efforts went futile. Puliyudaiyan was in utmost rage that he couldn't identify his daughter and started to attack her. Puliyavalli, being his daughter, could only block or evade his attacks.

Seeing Puliyavalli weakening, Shenba told Sureya to search on her own and he would help Puliyavalli. Shenba came in defense for Puliyavalli and entered in between her and her father.

As time went by, Puliyudaiyan didn't get tired, but his attacks got stronger. Realizing he couldn't beat the King, Shenba started to use his magic powers, but he got a huge blow from Puliyudaiyan. After a tiresome search, Sureya found her quest item.

"I found the *Olai Chuvadi*!" she screamed and ran back towards them. Puliyudaiyan, noticing the shout of excitement, leaped at Sureya with the sword pointing at her. Before anyone could realize anything the sword pierced through, with the sound of blood splashing.

There was still silence in that room. Shenba couldn't believe his eyes on what he was seeing. A voice murmured, "Father!"

On hearing those words, Puliyudaiyan regained his senses and saw the sword which he was holding. It was then he realized that he had stabbed his own daughter.

She fell in front of Sureya to save her. Puliyudaiyan removed his hand from the sword and started sobbing. He lifted his daughter and laid her over his lap and bawled.

Shenba came and stood near Sureya. Puliyavalli in her dying breath asked Shenba to fulfill their quest purpose. Puliyudaiyan stopped him and told those who revert the magic must receive the sacrament.

Sureya came forward to do it saying she must atone for her sins. Sureya read the *Olai Chuvadi*. As she started to read, there were heavy rumblings all around the palace. Every tiger-person started to come to their senses. Those who were locked up in the prison in the spiritual form slowly changed to physical form.

Meanwhile, Sureya was turning into a spiritual form. When

the reading was complete, Puliyudaiyan looked at her daughter. She was long gone. Sureya turned completely into a spirit.

The rumblings stopped. Puliyudaiyan got up and lifted his daughter and asked Shenba and Sureya to follow him to the courtroom. As they moved there was total agony and pain everywhere.

All the tiger-men and women were recovering from their loss of body parts and their friends' souls. When they saw their King, everyone ran towards him. Seeing Puliyavalli's body increased the roar which echoed throughout the palace.

Puliyudaiyan came to the center of the courtroom and placed his daughter's corpse there. Then he closed his eyes and murmured something. Then, the corpse started to float up slowly in the air.

Then, he made some gestures towards his guards. They immediately understood the King's commands and went away. After a few minutes, they came back with all the missing people from the village.

Among them were the Inspector, Tharanga Rajan, Indrakumar, Mannaiyan and Maadammal, and so on. Tharanga Rajan and Inspector came and hugged Shenba in their joy overwhelmingly.

Mannaiyan couldn't recognise Shenba but Shenba identified all of them. Tharanga Rajan whispered to others about Shenba. They were all exhilarated. Now, Puliyudaiyan started to speak in a loud voice. He said:

I, Puliyudaiyan, the King of Tiger People and Guardian of the Tiger Palace, have failed in my duty to protect my people from all kinds of danger, and have been a root cause of one such danger.

Hearing that everyone shouted, "No!" But he continued:

In the process of saving my people, I had forgone my duties to bring peace between humans and tigers. My major mistake was killing Soodammal's husband and cursing her.

Saying that he brought the spirit of Soodammal's husband and even turned her into her original physical form. Seeing his sister and her husband, Mannaiyan ran towards her and cried at her feet. Maadammal tried to console him. Then, the King said:

Today, I have lost my beloved daughter, Puliyavalli. I couldn't further bear any kind of loss. So, I have decided to move our palace to another realm where we could continue our lives peacefully. A place where we all were born.

Whispers could be heard everywhere around the court hall. Puliyudaiyan continued his oration:

This decision has been taken by me with a heavy heart. As a King, and as a common living being, I cannot court to any kind of war with anyone anymore. These many years, my beloved people, you have followed me with any orders I gave you. But this, you have to decide on your own whether to follow me or not. Because in the other realm, we would be in the complete tiger form with the memory of this world and this realm. Here, in this realm, you would be bestowed upon with the same powers you possess now but with no palace to protect you, you would be at the risk of getting attacked more. At some point, you would become the habitats of the realms which you chose. The realms would again meet after the completion of this yuga. Until then you would have to live here.

Now there was utter silence amongst the crowd. Few raised their hands and told the King that they would stay in this world's realm. Slowly, the tiger-people started taking sides as per the realms they chose. A bunch of Tiger-people opted to stay in the human realm.

When the question of their safety was aroused, few villagers from prisoners came forward saying they would protect them as their neighbours. Then all the villagers agreed in unison. Now, a teary smile appeared on a few faces on both sides.

Even, the King smiled acknowledging that peace had been made between humans and tiger people. Still, he worried about their safety a bit. Sensing the King's thought, Shenba came forward to protect them magically. The rest of the people assured the King that they would use everything in their possession to protect those tiger-people.

Even the Inspector came forward saying he would protect them by law. That raised the hopes of everyone. Then, the King said:

Now seeing that what was required had been fulfilled, We must depart to our realm where we belong. This peace has been brought by you, Shenba Nagulan. So, I bestow upon you all of my magical powers and knowledge over everything and also present you with my sword. Always use it to uphold justice and truth to whoever needs it.

The King took his sword and placed it in his open arms and gave it to Shenba. Shenba received the sword by bending on one knee and said, "Thank you, your Highness."

Sureya also thanked Shenba and gave all her knowledge and powers to him. Then the King said:

Though you hold the sword and the knowledge to use it, only regular practice would help you to master it. Now, you people, you are also my citizens. Hence you all would share all the wealth of this palace and you may lead a happy prosperous and peaceful life. Let's meet again in the spirit realm after your death.

Saying that he clapped his hands over his head which created a loud bang and a bright light. The next moment everything was gone. All the prisoners and the tiger people who chose to live in the human realm stood on the banks of the lake.

Now, there were few caves formed in the place of the palace. The Tiger people said this would be their home hereafter. Each and everyone who came out of the palace had magical objects and treasures at their feet. Shenba chanted and made the caves disappear.

When the magical objects were held, the caves became visible similar to the palace. All the villagers said that they didn't need any of those treasures. They said that they would build a temple for Puliyudaiyan in that place and keep all the treasures inside them.

They vowed to use it only when deemed necessary. The tiger people and the villagers parted their ways. As they started to move, Tharanga Rajan asked Shenba how he came there. Shenba explained about the letter brought by Mannaiyan and told about those scars.

Mannaiyan was dumbfounded by that and when he looked at his hands, all those scars were gone. It was the same with everyone who had scars. Seeing the Inspector's confusion, Shenba asked him. Inspector said that he had no idea how to close the case and asked Shenba for guidance.

Shenba laughed and nodded affirmatively. Everyone slowly moved towards Parangikadu as the sun started to rise and shine its light rays on the evergreen forest.

ABOUT THE AUTHOR

Vivek is an Engineer and an aspiring filmmaker who wrote this story for a script but published it. His years with his father, Mr. Elumalai who used to teach grammar to his brother, Mr. Vasanth, during his fourth grade and his brother's college days, inspired him to write English. He wrote his first story when he was in fourth grade for his school's silver jubilee magazine, which prompted him to embark on his writing journey. He also loves to write poems in both English and Tamil.

ACKNOWLEDGEMENTS

First of all, I would like to thank my father, Late. Mr. S. Elumalai, who was the Headmaster of a Government High School. He made a lot of things possible, which would have been difficult. I would like to express my gratitude to him for enabling me to study in English Medium.

I would also like to thank my mother, Mrs. D. Vijayalakshmi, who too, was the Headmistress of a Government Higher Secondary School. She supported me in my endeavours when I was stopped by my father. After my father's demise, she had supported us well and ensured that I didn't grieve my father's absence.

Next, I wish to thank my younger brother, Mr. E. Dharaneendiran, who is pursuing his Master's in Chemistry. He has been a wonderful companion in almost all of my efforts throughout my life.

Now, I would like to thank my cousins, Mr. B. Ashok Kumar, who got placed in the Health Department for service amidst this pandemic. He was my first support-system in my family.

Then, I thank Mr. M. Vasanth, who is now working as an English Teacher in a Panchayat Union Middle School. He was the key person in my life who inspired me to watch movies. He used to narrate the stories he wrote whenever I met him.

Next, I would like to thank Mr. V. Ranjith, who is now working as a Bus Conductor in Metropolitan Transport Corporation, Chennai. He was a father figure to me and my brother as we grew up. We spent more time with him than any other member of our family.

Now, I would like to thank Mrs. T. Sumathi and her student Mr. Balachandar for being there for me whenever I fought with my father about my grades, hobbies, etc.

Now, I thank the love of my life, my irritating companion, my stark contrast, who helps me to nullify everything and maintain the balance in life - my wife, Mrs. S. Sarguna. When we first met, my mother declared that she was looking for a daughter-in-law who would be a full-time housewife. I half expected people to take offense, but they agreed to my mom's request. On our next visit, I asked her if she would be okay with complying with my mother's demands, to which she said that she would happily continue doing what she was doing in her own household. At that time, I neither had any job nor a proper earning, yet she accepted me for who I was. She also allowed me to pursue my interest in movies. I can't thank her enough for the full, untiring support.

I would also like to extend my gratitude to my in-laws for accepting me as the ideal match for their daughter, and my cousin sisters Ms. V. Indhu and Ms. B. Naveena, who would always try to joke around even in dire situations, and make the atmosphere lighter.

Now, as of my friends, first, I would like to thank my friend again, Mrs. S. Vaisali, who inspired and persuaded me to write this book. Next, I would like to thank Mrs. R. Pavithra, initial editor of this book. When I started to send the pdf copies through WhatsApp, she used to read everything word by word and took the liberty of correcting my errors in writing.

Now, I would like to thank Mr. V. Praveen Kumar who works as a Marketing Executive in HDFC Bank, RS Puram, Coimbatore. He did whatever I asked as long as he could, even though he didn't like it.

I must also thank Mr. K. Srinivasan, who used to advise me in all my efforts and correct me, whenever I needed it.

Not to forget, I express my heartfelt gratitude to Mr. S. Vigneswaran, who used to feed me with his hard-earned money when I was in Coimbatore. There were days when we used to eat only once a day, which he provided despite financial trouble.

I thank Mr. A. Yeshwanth, who used to mock me at every possible step during my college days and encouraged me whenever I got sad. He encouraged me to take up coaching classes for the GATE Exam when he heard that I had applied for it. He would also give some suggestions to my writings.

Now, I must thank the two gangs from my hometown, Gingee, and my school town, Tindivanam were my driving force after my college days.

My Gingee Gang includes Clinton, Santhana Bharathi, Vinoth Kumar, Arun Padmanaban, S. Arun Kumar, and Matha - Mr. D. Clinton Joseph Raj, for constantly supporting and encouraging others to do so, Mr. V. Santhana Bharathi for being the mischief and joy of our gang, Mr. P. Vinoth Kumar for always understanding my point of view when reasoned with, Mr. Arun Padmanaban a UPSC and TNPSC aspirant, Mr. S. Arun Kumar, my childhood friend and an animator who would update me about the new upcoming in the Animation and Movie industry, and last but not the least, Mr. B. Mathan and Bharathi, my two long-lasting childhood friends.

My Tindivanam Gang includes Adarsh, Sivaraman, Mohan Raj, V. Praveen Kumar, Gokila, Pavithra, Girija, and Padmakumar. Mr. Adarsh was the coordinator of our gang. Mr.

R. Sivaraman is the person who persuaded me to pursue Animation in the first place when we were about to write our public exams in the tenth grade. Mr. R. Mohan Raj works on a ship. Mr. V. Praveen Kumar is another person from the Coimbatore guy. Since they both had the same names and initials, I had to add extra details to the previous guy. This fella would always tease me just like Yeshwanth maybe even more. As all our gang members would be out of station due to their jobs, most of the time only we would meet. He always wanted me to settle down so fast with a proper job and would render his help always.

Mrs. G. Gokila is the starter for all our get-togethers. When I and Sivaraman would talk about Hollywood movies, she would be the first person to get irritated. Because she doesn't watch them except on some occasions.

Ms. Girija being a doctor always absconds from the gang without any contact for years. When we started to think that she had forgotten us she would suddenly come out of nowhere and get in touch with us.

Mr. N. Padmakumar still doesn't have a WhatsApp account which makes us more trouble to reach him. He and his brother, Udhayanan gave me shelter and food during the time of Chennai International Film Festival - 2018. Sometimes we used to assume his brother was more friendly and frank than him to me and Mohan.

Now, I have to mention a few more people who made me into the person that I am today. They are Mr. E. Elangovan, who introduced me to Athiyan Anna and advised me to read as many books as possible. He would also often scrutinize me for my development in both knowledge and experience. He presented me with a screenplay book of a Rajnikanth movie, Johnny written and directed by Mahendran. The second person is Mr. Sadesh who would always introduce me to a wide range of new movies and offer company for film festivals. The third one is Mr. Suresh Kumar who offers his opinion about my works.

I also would like to thank Mr. Vadivel and his sister Mrs. Sangeetha who would offer me Computer Services with much care and encourage me in my endeavours and support me technically.

I thank Mr. Athiyan Athirai who gave me a deep insight saying, "No matter what film you watch or what book you read, you would end up making a movie with what you like. So, don't ask which movie to watch or which book to read. Repeat the process for even the same movie or same book, you would always learn a new thing every time."

I must thank my owner Mr. Hem Kumar for his support. And my colleagues Mr. Manikandan and Mr. Durai for sharing and helping me in work when I was a newbie.

I also must thank Mr. Dheeban Raja to whom I made acquaintance with and who told me to develop a screenplay based on the story which I intend to do. I also thank Mr. G.D. Albert, who first made a hardcopy of this book and encouraged me to publish it.

Last but not least, I must thank my teachers, particularly, two people. They are Rev. Bro. John Paul and Mrs. Anandhi. These two were my English teachers in Standards 7, 8, and 9, 10 respectively. They shaped my English into a better form and shape if not best as of today after my father. They used to beat the pulp out of us while teaching Grammar Classes. I would proudly say my English Language skill set is based on these three pillars.

Finally, I want to thank Inkfeathers Team for supporting me in the publishing process and Ms. Saranya Dhandapani, Author and Compiler of "Until Then There's Coffee" for introducing them to me.

Those who read all this by now must feel slight drowsiness. Fear not! It would fade momentarily. Some might wonder if I have missed their names. As I said earlier, if I have to thank and mention everyone in my life, I would have to publish another book. So, I settled with these periods of writing.

When and if I get a chance to write and share my whole life as a book or something related to you is processed in works, I would try to mention your names there. Until then, I apologize for the names that I have forgotten to mention in the book.